GIRL HERO

First American Edition 2015
Kane Miller, A Division of EDC Publishing

Cover illustrations by Dyani Stagg
Text, design and illustrations copyright © Lemonfizz Media 2010
First published by Scholastic Australia Pty Limited in 2010
This edition published under license from Scholastic Australia Pty
Limited on behalf of Lemonfizz Media

For information contact:
Kane Miller, A Division of EDC Publishing
P.O. Box 470663
Tulsa, OK 74147-0663
www.kanemiller.com
www.edcpub.com
www.usbornebooksandmore.com

Library of Congress Control Number: 2014949840

Printed and bound in the United States of America
3 4 5 6 7 8 9 10

ISBN: 978-1-61067-383-9

IN THE DARK

Kane Miller
A DIVISION OF EDC PUBLISHING

Chapter •1

It was night, and Emma Jacks was lying in bed wide-awake, feeling nervous. In fact, she was quite scared. The hall light was on, but it still seemed very dark to Emma, and Emma didn't like the dark. You couldn't see what was going on, and when you couldn't see what was going on, you sometimes imagined scary things.

Emma turned her bedside light on and that helped, sort of. There were still shadows and noises—and every noise she heard worried her.

Was the thing making the noise inside, was it outside? Was it outside but wanting to come inside? Was it something dangerous?

Part of Emma knew she was being silly, but the other half, slightly more than half, couldn't stop feeling scared. And once she started thinking about one scary thing, more things seemed to tumble into her head. At least she had already realized that the tall, pointy shadows that seemed to be coming toward her room from the hallway were only the coats hanging up on the coatrack. They were the same coats that hung there every day, so why did her imagination tell her that they might suddenly become something scary at night? It was the same with the dangerous shape on the end of her bed, the dangerous gymnastics bag that was always there. It was nuts.

Then Emma heard a bang. In seconds, she was out of bed, down the hallway and into the living room where her mom was watching television. Their little husky puppy, Pip, was snuggled on her mom's lap. Bang! There it was again. It came from the next room, the kitchen.

Mom looked up. "Sorry, Em. Dad's being a bit noisy with the trash can. Did the noise wake you?" she asked.

Oh, that was the trash can, Emma thought to herself. *That's embarrassing.*

"Um, no, I just wondered what that noise was, but now that I know, it's okay."

"Back to bed then," said Mom.

Emma was hoping her mom would say, "Why don't you cuddle up here and watch a bit of television first?" but it was a school night and that was unlikely to happen. She walked back down the hallway and had just reached her bedroom door when she saw a tall, dark figure standing in front of her closet. Emma froze, her mouth went dry, she felt her heart beat fast and her mind started racing faster. What was it and what was it doing in her bedroom? Was it looking for her? Quickly she turned on the light…*Oh, it is my "evil" bathrobe*, thought Emma, relieved but also embarrassed, even if there was no one else around.

This is ridiculous, thought Emma, as she got back into bed. *Get a grip, Emma! Are you afraid of your bathrobe now?* She lay there, eyes wide-open, thinking. Why did she always get so jumpy in the dark? How was she going to cope at Hannah's slumber party if she got this nervous in her own bed? Did the other girls feel scared sometimes?

Emma started counting backward from one thousand. Sometimes that helped her get to sleep because it was so boring. *1000, 999, 998, 997, 996, 995, maybe I need a glass of water, 994, 993, 992, yes, I think I do, 991 990, 989, 988, okay, I'll go and get one.*

Emma walked back down the hallway. Both Mom and Dad were watching television now. She slipped into the room without them noticing and stopped just behind the sofa. Maybe if she stayed quiet she could sit there for a while, undetected, and watch a little television to take her mind off things? *Good idea, Em*, she thought. *No one will know I'm here.*

Wrong.

Pip must have heard her. The puppy jumped off

the sofa, saw Emma sitting behind it and, delighted that her play friend was up again, bounded around her licking her face. Emma spluttered. Loudly.

"Emma, is that you? Why aren't you in bed?" Mom sounded slightly irritated.

"I just needed a glass of water."

"And there's one behind the sofa?"

"Oh, um, well I saw what you were watching and thought I might…"

"Back to bed you go," said Mom. "You need to go to sleep or you will be grumpy and tired for school in the morning. You can take Pip with you to keep you company."

So Emma and Pip walked back to her room. Emma checked under her bed and in her night table and then under her bed again just to make sure, then she jumped under the covers. Pip jumped in too, taking up her secret position under the quilt next to Emma. Her dad would have a fit if he saw her. He would declare it, "a hygiene issue."

The sound of the television from the living room made Emma feel closer to her parents and with Pip snuggled next to her on one side and her favorite soft toy, Floppy, on the other, it was quite cozy. It was best to keep Floppy and Pip separate. Pip loved Floppy in a chew toy kind of way. Emma felt comfy, sleepy even, and her eyes slowly closed. Then from outside there was a rustling. Then a noise.

Hiiiiiiiiiiiiiiiiiiiiiiiiiiiiissssssssssssssssssssss!

Emma's eyes shot wide-open and she froze. *Gee whizz, lemonfizz, what was that?*

Hiiiiiiiiiiiiiiiiiiiiiiiiiiiiiiiiissssssssssssssssssssssssss!

There it was again. Emma didn't wait to hear it a third time. She jumped out of bed and ran back into the living room. Pip, thinking this was a hilarious new game, scampered behind her, barking.

"Em?" said Mom in a decidedly irritated voice.

"Why are you up again?" asked Dad.

"There's something right outside my window," said Emma breathlessly. "Something really noisy, something really angry. I think it is trying to get in."

"Emma, are you…"

Hiiiiiiiiiiiiiiiiiiiiiiiiiiiiiiiisssssssssssssssssssssssssssss!

Emma jumped onto the sofa between her parents. "There it is again!" she squealed. "Mom, what are we going to do?"

"It's okay, Emma," said Mom. "That's a possum."

"That is *not* a possum," said Emma, fearing her mom had gone completely crazy. "Possums are cute, they have little pink noses, they nibble on things. The thing outside making that noise is some mean creature that's coming to attack us."

"No, Em, really, it's a possum," said Mom, almost laughing. "They make those noises to scare predators away."

"It certainly scared me."

"Why don't we go outside with a flashlight and find it so you can see for yourself?"

They went outside and Emma's mom shone the flashlight onto the back fence. Sure enough, halfway along the fence was a ring-tailed possum with big eyes and a long tail with a white tip. The possum was sitting perfectly still, staring unblinking at Emma and her mom. Much to Emma's delight, a baby possum was clinging to the possum's back.

"See," said Mom, "a possum, two possums actually." She turned off the flashlight and the possum scuttled along the fence and up a tree.

"They were soooooo cute," said Emma. "How can something so cute make such a horrible noise?" Emma felt a bit silly. She wondered if they had possums at Hannah's house. She was starting to think about other noises that might scare her at the slumber party when her mom interrupted her thoughts.

"Look up," said Mom. "It's a beautiful star-bright night."

Emma looked up. It was true. Stars were flickering, like twinkling lights, all over the black night sky.

"Maybe another night we can do some star-gazing," said her mom, "but now it's back into bed, madam."

This time Mom came with Emma to the bedroom, tucked her into bed and gave her a big hug. "Sleep tight, my little one," she whispered in Emma's ear.

Emma snuggled down again, too tired to be scared anymore. *Little one is right, silly little one,* thought Emma. *I can go on missions all over the world and I am afraid of the dark? What would A1 say if she knew?*

But before she could answer that, she was, finally, asleep.

Chapter •2

A1 was the head of the **SHINE** agency, a secret organization that protected the world from evildoers. "We shine a light on evil," was one of their mottoes. (**SHINE** liked mottoes and they had one for most things.) They spent a lot of time shining a light on the *SHADOW* agency, uncovering and stopping their evil plans. *SHADOW* was as bad as **SHINE** was good.

What did all this have to do with Emma Jacks? Well, when she wasn't worrying about strange noises at night, or going to school or gymnastics or playing with her friends or being irritated by her older brother, Bob, and other normal ten-year-old girl things, Emma Jacks was EJ12. EJ12, special agent and code-cracker, under-twelve division, to be exact (which Emma liked to be). In fact, she was one of **SHINE's** best agents. In the agency's Shining Stars award, **SHINE's** Spy of the Year competition, EJ12 was in the top five.

Emma had been selected to join **SHINE** when she won a math competition. **SHINE** used math competitions as a way of finding clever thinkers to help them crack codes, and they had found Emma. Since then, as EJ12, she had cracked codes and gone on missions all over the world. As EJ12, Emma Jacks seemed to be able to do anything.

So how could a special agent be afraid of the dark? So far EJ12 had only been sent on day missions. She didn't know it, but that was about to change.

"Emma, time to wake up," said her mom, as she pulled up the blind in Emma's bedroom.

Emma opened her eyes. The sunlight rushed into the bedroom and made her squint. She dived under her quilt. "Mom, pull down the blind pleeeeeease, it's too light!"

"That's a first," said Mom, as she left the room. "You normally want more light. Come on, sleepy head, let's get moving."

Emma was tired. The problem with staying up late worrying about dangerous bathrobes and strange noises was that you felt sleepy the next morning. But how different things were in the daylight—bathrobes went back to being bathrobes, gymnastics bags were gymnastics bags, and Emma wouldn't even think about checking under her bed.

Emma got dressed and went down to the kitchen. Mom, Dad and Bob were already there having breakfast.

"You'll both need to move quickly this morning," said Mom to Emma and Bob. "I need to be at work early so you will have to catch the bus. Hurry up, come on!"

Excellent, thought Emma. *Hannah and Elle will probably be on the bus.*

And to Emma's delight, Hannah and Elle *and* Isi were on the bus. Isi was on Emma's gymnastics team, but Emma was only getting to know her more now that they were in the same class at school. Emma really liked Isi. They liked a lot of the same things, particularly chocolate, and Isi was always cheerful and seemed to bounce her way through everything. Emma wondered if Isi ever got scared of the dark. She didn't think so.

As the bus pulled up to the stop, Emma could see her friends peering out the window, waving frantically. As soon as Emma climbed on, the three girls started talking at her.

"Hey, Em, we were hoping you'd catch the bus today. We've been talking about my slumber party," said Hannah.

"We're thinking we should have a theme," said Elle.

"Em, Em, it's going to be sooo fun," said Isi.

"Hi, guys. A theme is a great idea," said Emma, "but what theme?"

"First we thought a dance party," said Hannah.

"That would be cool," agreed Emma.

"Then we thought a pajama party," said Isi.

"But won't we be in pajamas anyway?" asked Emma, who was very logical.

"Exactly, that's what we thought," said Isi, "so then we had a better idea—a spooky slumber party!"

"Oh," said Emma, trying to sound as if that was a good surprise rather than a completely bad surprise. "What would we do for that?"

"It would be awesome, Em," said Elle. "We can tell ghost stories, have a midnight feast . . ."

"And play 'murder in the dark' outside," broke in Hannah.

"And watch scary movies!" shrieked Isi, who was so excited she was nearly falling off her seat. "What do you think, Em? How cool will that be?"

"Yeah, but a dance party could be really fun too," said Emma, looking at Hannah.

Hannah smiled back. "Spooky will be fun, Em,

don't you think?"

"Oh, I don't know," said Emma, but she did know and if she couldn't tell these friends what she was thinking, who could she tell? "What if we get scared?"

"That's the point, dummy," said Elle.

"No, I mean *really* scared," said Emma.

"Don't worry," said Hannah, putting her arm around Emma. "We'll look after you."

But Emma wasn't convinced. She loved her friends and wanted to join in but was fairly sure she would be really, really scared at a spooky slumber party. Perhaps she shouldn't go.

The bus pulled into school. The girls got out and as they walked into the school grounds they saw Alisha walking in as well. Isi bounded up to her and Elle shouted, "Alisha, Alisha, over here!"

Alisha ran over, colliding with Isi who gave her a big hug in typical Isi style.

"Alisha, you'll never guess what we thought of for Hannah's slumber party—a spooky party."

"Cool," said Alisha. "I could bring my glow-in-the-dark mask."

Oh excellent, thought Emma. *Not.* Why was everyone so keen to be scared? Was Emma the only one who got scared and *didn't* find it fun? She bet Alisha loved creeping around in the dark in her glowing mask.

At lunchtime, the girls were still talking about the slumber party, thinking of even more ways they could scare themselves. Emma had been looking forward to the slumber party, but now she wasn't sure she wanted to go. She was getting scared just talking about it. What would the others think if she got scared? She knew Hannah and Elle wouldn't make fun of her, but would Isi and Alisha think she was a baby? She really liked her new friends, but would they still like her if they thought she was a scaredy-cat?

Piinngg!

The sudden sound made Emma jump, but she pulled her phone out of her pocket and saw the screen flashing, a nice aqua flash. Aqua was Emma's favorite color and an aqua flash on her phone could mean only one thing—a mission alert from SHINE.

Chapter 3

SHINE used special text messages to let their agents know when they were needed for a new mission. That meant the agents needed to have a phone, which was great if you were an agent who had been having problems convincing your parents you needed one. Emma thought her phone was simply the coolest phone ever. It was a cross between a game console and a touch screen phone, with lots of applications, many of them top secret SHINE apps that were hidden behind the more usual ones. There were apps to identify wild animals, apps to help you crack codes, even apps about apps, and SHINE was always inventing new ones to help their agents. The phone also had lots of games. Emma's current favorite was Jump Start, where the girl has to jump from jungle vine to vine to collect fruit to feed a baby monkey. But there was no time for games now. Emma needed to report in to SHINE.

"I'll see you later," said Emma to her friends. "I've just got to check on something."

"Okay, Em, see you later," said Hannah, and she smiled. She was used to Emma suddenly leaving.

Emma hurried over to the bathroom. Once inside, she turned on the hand dryers and checked that no one else was there. With the room clear, she headed for the last stall on the right and pushed the door open. She went in and locked the door. Emma put down the toilet seat, sat down and flipped open the toilet paper holder where there was, as you would expect, toilet paper. There was also, if you knew what to look for, the SHINE Mission Tube access socket. The SHINE Mission Tube was a secret tunnel transportation system that carried agents to

SHINE HQ and other top secret **SHINE** locations. Each agent had a home tunnel, or in Emma's case a school tunnel, which meant agents could move quickly once they received a mission alert. Carefully disguised in unexpected locations, the Mission Tube's entrance points were almost impossible to detect. Emma understood that it was important for the Mission Tube to be top secret, but did it really have to start in the girls' bathroom? Emma thought not.

Emma pushed her phone into the socket and waited. There was a beep then Emma entered her pin code and removed her phone. Another beep and then the usual message flashed up on her phone screen.

WELCOME BACK EJ12.

EJ loved the next bit. Suddenly, the wall behind the toilet spun around, with the toilet and EJ still attached. EJ slipped off the toilet seat and onto a beanbag at the top of what looked like a giant tunnel slide. This was the start of the **SHINE** Mission Tube. A protective shield came over the back of the beanbag, covering EJ. The wall then spun back and EJ heard the click as the stall door unlocked on the other side. Everything in the stall would seem completely normal.

EJ was ready. She typed "go" into her phone and…

WHOOOOOOOOOSH

Traveling down the tube and into the **SHINE** tube network, EJ whizzed around corners at high speed. This time, however, the lights along the tube seemed dimmer than usual, making it darker and casting shadows on the usually bright steel walls. EJ normally loved the Mission Tube ride, but this time it was less fun somehow. She was almost relieved when she slowed to a halt at a small platform with a keypad and screen. The protective shield over the beanbag flipped back and EJ again keyed in her pin code and waited for the security check.

The check changed each time. Sometimes it was an eye scan, sometimes voice matching, once it was big toe recognition. You never knew what it would be—and neither would anyone attempting to break into the SHINE network.

"Please place hand on pad," requested a digital voice.

Hmmm, this is a new one, thought Emma, as she followed the instructions.

EJ put her left hand onto the pad.

"Incorrect placement," said the voice.

EJ frowned and jiggled her hand around.

"Correct placement confirmed but incorrect hand. Please place writing hand on pad," said the voice.

"Well, why didn't you say so?" said EJ, feeling a little irritated and then a little silly for talking to a computer-generated voice. EJ put her right hand on the pad.

"Correct hand, correct placement now confirmed," said the voice. "Please wait. Handprint scan in progress."

Phew, thought Emma.

There was a short, sharp flash on the pad then a low buzzing noise. After a few seconds, there was another flash.

"Handprint scan is now complete. Agent identity confirmed. Please drop in, EJ12!"

There was another beep as the platform beneath her opened up and EJ, still on her beanbag, dropped gently down. She had landed in the Code Room, a small chamber where there was a table, a chair and a clear plastic tube protruding from the ceiling. EJ moved to the chair and waited.

She heard the familiar whizzing noise, put her hands under the tube and caught a little capsule that popped out. EJ opened the capsule and took out a piece of paper and a pen. She could feel the butterflies starting to flutter inside her as they always did when she was getting a new code. They were good butterflies, exciting, the sort you got when you were waiting to open a present. Emma read the message on the paper.

For EJ12's Eyes Only

Message intercepted from SHADOW 12.46.

Sent to EJ12 12.51.

Urgent decode required.

EJ looked at the paper. There seemed to be nothing under this information. *Invisible ink again maybe*, she thought, and activated her Invisi-Visi app and a small purple light flashed on her phone. It was ultraviolet that would show up invisible ink. She scanned the paper with the ray, expecting to see a message appear. It didn't.

What now? thought EJ.

EJ fiddled with her charm bracelet as she often did when she was thinking, and looked at the paper again. This time, however, she not only looked really closely at the piece of paper, she felt it carefully. She ran her fingers up and down the page. As she did, she noticed that there were little bumps all over the paper. Was that just the texture of the paper or was it something else? Could it be part of the message?

EJ felt the little bumps again and then had an idea. She took a pen out of her backpack and carefully drew a black dot on top of each bump. When she finished she looked at the piece of paper—there were dots everywhere, but they seemed to be in a pattern.

For EJ12's Eyes Only

Message intercepted from SHADOW 12.46.

Sent to EJ12 12.51.

Urgent decode required.

I think I recognize that, said EJ to herself. *I wonder if it is Braille, the writing invented for blind people?*

Let's check. EJ took out her phone, touched on her code app and flicked through until she found the Braille alphabet then pressed "OK." The Braille alphabet flashed onto her screen, looking the same as the dot patterns on the paper.

A	B	C	D	E	F	G	H
I	J	K	L	M	N	O	P
Q	R	S	T	U	V	W	X
Y	Z						

Okay, thought EJ, *let's get this code cracked.*

Carefully, EJ began matching the code to the key. She quickly got the first two words, writing them under the code.

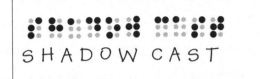

SHADOW CAST

Looks like it is a straightforward Braille code, thought EJ. *This should be easy.*

And it was. Well, for an expert code-cracker anyway. EJ had the code out in minutes.

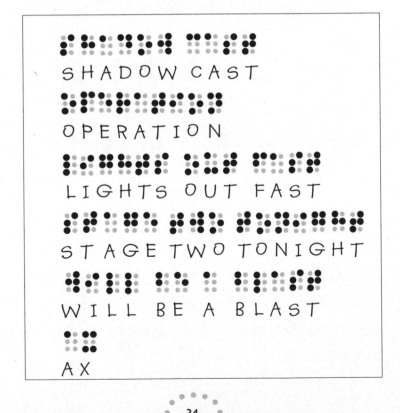

SHADOW CAST

OPERATION

LIGHTS OUT FAST

STAGE TWO TONIGHT

WILL BE A BLAST

A X

The message may have been decoded, but what did it mean? EJ12 would have to get help to answer that question. She folded the paper with the decoded message on it and slid it back into the capsule. She then pushed the capsule back up the tube and it was sucked away. The message would shoot back to **SHINE HQ**, which was where EJ needed to go. She keyed "go" into her keypad. The floor under her beanbag slipped back and she dropped down into another tube, which would take her there. The tube was even darker than before. What was going on?

Chapter 4

Things were also not as EJ expected them to be when she arrived in the **SHINE HQ** operations room. Instead of the usual bright lights and flashing screens, the room was dim and shadowy. Only a few monitors were on and there were candles burning at each workstation.

"It is all a bit dark and dingy here, I'm afraid, but welcome back, EJ12," said A1, who was, as always, there to greet EJ. A1's large, bright-yellow pendant, the one she always wore, seemed even brighter in the gloomy room.

"But why is it so dark?" asked EJ. "And why was it so dark in the Mission Tube?"

"We're trying to save power because we are running low," said A1. "All of SHINE's power comes from our own solar energy plant," she explained. "We wouldn't be a very secret secret organization if we had to use the normal energy supply, so we make our own. The plant is in an isolated location, known to only a few people. Over the last week the energy levels have been slowly dropping. We don't know why."

"Perhaps something has broken at the plant," suggested EJ.

"That's what we thought at first, but our head engineer herself has checked all the machinery. Twice. Everything is in perfect working order."

"Then maybe there has been less sunlight?" said EJ.

"We checked that as well. For the last week there have been perfect conditions, almost ridiculously clear blue skies," said A1. "Let's hope the message you decoded shines some light on the problem."

Normally at this point in a mission meeting with A1, the enormous Light Screen would lower. The Light Screen was like the **SHINE** brain, connecting all the files stored on the **SHINE** network with information from all over the web and the world. Images would flash up, maps would appear, and videos and audio would play on the Light Screen, all helping **SHINE** to piece together the puzzle of a *SHADOW* plot. The Light Screen was normally lowered by voice command using electricity, but now A1 was pulling it down like a blind and, rather than all those screens, it was just a whiteboard. EJ wasn't impressed and must have looked it.

"I know, EJ, it's not as impressive as usual, but the Light Screen uses much too much power," said A1. "We have to save it for when we really need it. Right, let's get down to work."

"Okay," replied EJ, trying to sound enthusiastic. "We can start with the code."

"Indeed, EJ," said A1. "Let's put that up on the board." A1 took up a marker pen and began to write…

EJ thought A1's handwriting was beautiful. She wished she could write like that.

> *Shadow Cast*
>
> *Operation*
>
> *Lights Out Fast*
>
> *Stage Two Tonight*
>
> *Will Be A Blast*
>
> *AX*

"Good work on decoding the message so quickly, EJ12. Now we need to work out what it means. I wonder why they used Braille?"

"Maybe the person who wrote it is blind," suggested EJ.

"Or the person who was being sent the message," said A1.

"Or maybe the message had to be read in the dark."

"Yes, quite. It could be for any reason—or just be something to trick us. What is certain is that Operation Lights Out is behind our decreasing energy supplies. And the message says 'Operation Lights Out Fast.' If that means what I think it does, then the operation is moving quickly and we are in trouble."

"But what *is* Operation Lights Out?" asked EJ. "What is Stage Two and who do you think is behind it all? And why does the message rhyme?"

"It's very bad rhyming though, isn't it?" said A1. "But the code gives us some clues. Look, SHADOW CAST, casting a shadow on our light supplies. That confirms that it is *SHADOW*. They've tried before to attack our power supplies and they love using clever names for their plans. But who is sending this report to them about Operation Lights Out? Who is behind this evil scheme? It must be one of their scientists, but which one?"

"Whoever they are, they like poetry," EJ pointed out. "And the message ends with the letters AX—are they the initials of the person sending the message?"

"AX," said A1. "Could it be, I wonder?" And for

a moment A1 looked deep in thought, her brow crumpling as she frowned.

"A1?" said EJ. She wished she knew what A1 was thinking.

"Yes, yes, my turn to wander off, sorry, EJ12," replied A1. "We'll run the initials through the **SHINE** records. Because we're working with such low energy it will take some time. We will have to text you the results. In the meantime we need to text you where they are operating from. We'll need a map."

Usually A1 would speak to the voice activated Light Screen and a map would appear. She might then say, "Find solar plant" and the Light Screen would hone in on the location, combining 3-D mapping with satellite photography to show possible locations and the best routes to get there. Instead, A1 opened a cupboard and took out a large roll of paper, blowing dust off it as she unrolled it on a table.

"This is a map of the area around our power station, EJ. It's quite deserted, but over a hundred years ago, it was a busy gold-mining area. There's an old mine somewhere north of the bushland, past the station, if I am not mistaken…"

A1 is never mistaken, thought EJ.

A1 bent over the map with her fingers following one pathway and then another until…"Aha! There it is," she said sticking a pin into the map. "'Black Cave Mine—abandoned' it says here. Let's see if we can find out more."

"With the Light Screen this time?" asked EJ hopefully.

"No, EJ, with a book about the area's history," said A1. "We had our books scanned, but we also kept the originals. Stand back," and with that A1 pushed a button and the wall behind her flipped around, monitor and all. Floor to ceiling bookshelves were on the other side. With the candlelight, the wooden bookcases and dusty books, the **SHINE** Operations Room suddenly looked less like a twenty-first-century spy center and more like an old-fashioned library.

Weird but also cool, thought EJ.

"It might be up here," called A1 from the top

of a long ladder on wheels that could move from bookcase to bookcase. "Let me look, geography, no, no, here, the history section. Now we need the book for that area. Here!" A1 pulled out the book and passed it down to EJ. "See what you can find."

EJ turned to the index. She flicked from A to C then back to B. Then she ran her finger down the columns as she looked through the B entries. The Light Screen would have found the answer in seconds. *Hmm*, she thought, as she read, *Ballroom Dancing, Birds…Black Cave Mine.* "A1, I've found it."

"Brilliant, EJ. What does the book say about it?"

EJ checked the page number then flicked to the page. She did think googling the mine would have been easier.

"We don't need Google, EJ12," said A1.

There she goes again, thought EJ.

"This book will tell us what we need and we can save the power," continued A1. "Read it out loud now, in a big loud voice."

"Okay," said EJ and she began reading. "'The

Black Cave Mine was one of the largest gold mines in the area. It was named for the dark tunnel system built as the miners searched for gold. Mine carts running on tracks were used to carry rock and gold out of the mine's numerous entrances. On top of the hill, a mine tower stood above the mine shaft—a large hole running from the top to the bottom of the mine—that linked all the tunnels to the top of the mine. A simple elevator system in the mine shaft raised and lowered a large metal cage on wires running from the top of the mine tower. It was used to lower supplies into the mine and as another exit for the miners. The mine was abandoned at the end of the nineteenth century, but the tower still stands on what is now known as Black Cave Hill.' And, look, A1," said EJ showing her the page, "there's a drawing of the mine's tunnel system."

"Good work, EJ. Look at the picture closely. You can see the tunnels widen on either side of the shaft into little rooms. The miners used these landings to store equipment and supplies. We might find Operation Lights Out in one of those."

"Yes, but what *is* Operation Lights Out?" said EJ.

"That's what you need to find out, EJ12. *SHADOW* is up to something in that mine. Tonight they will be ready to go to the next stage—and I don't like the idea of it being a blast. Let's get you ready, EJ12." A1 picked up a candlestick and moved back to the briefing table. "We have a few new things for you."

EJ was excited. What clever inventions would **SHINE** have for her this time?

Chapter • 5

"This will be an underground operation, EJ," said A1.

"Well, we are a secret underground organization, A1," replied EJ.

"No, I mean that if we are right and Operation Lights Out is operating from the mine, you are going to have to go under the ground to find it."

EJ gulped. "Underground? Down into Black Cave Mine?"

"Yes, EJ," said A1. "Actually it won't make much difference to the mission if you are underground or above ground—you will be working at night."

A night mission? EJ suddenly felt less than excited. *Can I do this?* she wondered.

"You can do this, EJ12," said A1 loudly. "I know you can."

You might not be so sure, thought EJ, *if you knew that I get scared by my bathrobe or my gymnastics bag or if you realized how my imagination runs away with me, making me too scared to move.*

"The trick with night missions," said A1 firmly but kindly, "is not to let your imagination run away with you. Everything is exactly the same at night as it is in the daytime, just harder to see. 'Shine a light on your fears,' that's an old **SHINE** motto, you know. And lighten up, EJ12!" chuckled A1. "We've equipped you with everything you need, including a light pack." She passed EJ a backpack.

"This feels heavy," said EJ.

"Not a lightweight pack," said A1, laughing. "A bag of lights, different kinds of lights that will help you see. Take a look inside."

EJ unpacked the bag, laying everything out on the table. As she did, she began to feel a little more confident. There was a large flashlight, a small flashlight, night-vision glasses and even some candles and matches.

"Don't forget your boots, EJ," said A1. "They've been upgraded and I think they should give you a real lift."

EJ looked at the black boots on the table. "I don't suppose you've fixed the rather random way the boots work?" she asked. She was thinking back to her jungle mission when she clicked and ice skates appeared. Or when she was in Antarctica searching for the ice skates and she got flippers.

"Not quite, but you will be pleased to hear," said A1 quickly moving the conversation on, "that we have some new charms for your bracelet."

EJ's face brightened. She loved the **SHINE** charms. CHARM stood for Clever Hidden Accessories with Release Mechanism. **SHINE** wanted their agents to be able to carry their equipment with them easily and without attracting attention. The **SHINE** inventors created a process for shrinking things and inserting them into charms. The agent activated the equipment with a simple twist of the charm. It was incredible the things they thought of—there was spray to attract butterflies, sounds to repel crocodiles, ice picks, penguin food dispensers—*the SHINE inventors were clever women indeed*, thought EJ.

"The **SHINE** inventors are clever women, aren't they, EJ?" said A1.

This mind reading thing is getting a little weird, thought EJ.

"This time they have really outdone themselves," A1 said.

EJ looked at the four new charms: there was a twisted string, a ladybug, a sun and a little heart with a candle within it. "They're pretty," she said.

"And practical," said A1. She picked up the sun charm. "This is perhaps the most important one."

EJ looked closer and saw that it was glowing yellow. "That's beautiful," she exclaimed.

"It's more than just beautiful," said A1. "This charm has a transmitter which is linked to our power station's energy level monitor. The color changes according to the level: blue is normal, yellow is below normal, orange for well below normal, red for dangerously low and flashing red for near empty."

"Let's hope I don't see that one," said EJ. As she walked toward the **SHINE** dressing rooms to get ready, she attached the charms to her bracelet. Changing into her mission clothes always made EJ feel stronger, more confident. This time she was wearing head to toe black: black top, black cargo pants, black **SHINE** utility belt, even a black headband. **SHINE** thought of everything.

EJ checked her utility belt, which had all the usual things, such as binoculars, compass (glow-in-the-dark issue), pocketknife, phone holder and, this time, a little tub of what looked like black mud. EJ checked the label.

SHINE

FACE CONCEALER

Just a few smudges and no one will know you are there!

"What do I need this for?" EJ asked, as she came out of the dressing rooms.

"We want you to blend in with your surroundings, which you will if you are head to toe black. You will be as dark as the night—and the mine," said A1. EJ wished she hadn't reminded her. "But you won't be alone," said A1. "Remember to upload your BEST."

SHINE believed their agents worked better with backup, so they had developed the BEST agent assistance system. BEST stood for Brains, Expertise, Support, Tips and every agent had a network of people she could call on to help her. The BESTies, as they were known, were screened by SHINE HQ and cleared to help the agent on missions. They were there to support the agent when the mission got tough. The BESTies could ask no questions and an agent could never discuss her work with them when a mission was over. That was okay with the BESTies—they liked being part of a top secret mission, even if they couldn't tell anyone about it.

EJ opened the BEST app on her phone, flicked through her contacts and thought hard. Hannah,

Elle, Mom... Who would she need on this mission? It was hard to tell when the mission hadn't begun, but all the talk about darkness was scaring EJ a bit, and who did she turn to when she felt scared? Mom. EJ's mom had also been a **SHINE** agent so she knew how things worked. Yes, Mom would be perfect, decided EJ. EJ selected her mom on the screen and pressed "OK" to activate the BEST communication system. EJ's mom would now be alerted by text message that she had been selected as a mission BESTie. She would be advised to stay alert and be on standby should EJ need her. *That's funny*, thought EJ, *that's sort of what moms seem to do anyway.*

"Ready, EJ12?" asked A1. "It's time to get going. You will be taking the Mission Tube train. We use it to transport the engineers to the solar plant. The train line finishes just past the power station, a little way out in the bush. Once out of the Mission Tube, you will need to make your way north through the bush to the mine. Use your compass. Hopefully we will intercept another message which will give us some more clues to help you, but for now, good luck, EJ12," and with that A1 pushed a button under the briefing table. The wall at the end of the briefing room slid back to reveal the Mission Tube and a small, silver bullet train.

"Wow!" exclaimed EJ. "Has that been here the whole time?"

"Yes, EJ12. The beanbags work well for short trips, but if they travel too far along the mission tube, the bags begin to wear and the beans begin to fall out," explained A1. "And, of course, they can only carry one person at a time. That's where our bullet train comes in."

"But who is going to drive it?" asked EJ.

"You are, of course," replied A1.

"I am?" said EJ, looking surprised but also excited.

"I have checked your training reports and you did pretty well on the 'Steering-with-Speed' unit, so I know you will have no problems at all with the bullet train," said A1. "It is one of the easiest of all our trains to drive."

SHINE regularly held classes and workshops at

its top secret training base. It was like a camp for secret agents. **SHINE** needed to make sure that their agents were up-to-date with the very latest developments in code-cracking and knew how to use the equipment they were given on missions. EJ loved these camps and the Under-12 Driving Camp had been one of the best. She had been trained on lawn mowers (you never knew what might be needed on a mission), tractors, dirt bikes, snowmobiles, diggers and trains. The "Steering-with-Speed" part of the camp was the best as the agents practiced going as fast as they could while still keeping control of their vehicle. It was so much better than the bumper cars at the carnival.

"OK, EJ12, all aboard," said A1.

Excellent! thought EJ. *My brother would be so jealous if he knew.*

Chapter •6

The bullet train was easy to drive, and fun. EJ simply pushed a start button then pulled a lever up and down to control the speed. She remembered from her training that you sped through the straights and slowed down around the turns. It was better than the big dipper at the carnival. Except it was getting darker as the Mission Tube lights grew dimmer.

Piinngg!

It was a text message from **SHINE**. Had they intercepted another *SHADOW* message already?

POWER LEVELS
CONTINUE TO DROP.
REDUCING POWER TO
MISSION TUBE LIGHTS.
EMERGENCY LIGHTING
ONLY.

The emergency lighting was very dim. It was now nearly impossible to see the twists and turns of the tunnel and EJ slowed way down. After driving very slowly for a while, she checked her map app and saw that it was now straight ahead to the end of the line. *That's better*, she thought, as she pulled the lever up again and returned to full speed. Soon the console on the driving panel flashed "approaching line end." EJ pulled the lever slowly down, bringing the train to a halt in front of a ladder and a sign.

UP FOR EXIT

EJ pushed a large button by the train door. The door slid open and EJ stepped out of the train onto a narrow platform. She edged along the platform to the front of the train before climbing up onto the front of the train and onto the ladder. EJ then climbed up the ladder until she reached the top and a metal door above her, like a manhole. It had a bolt, two locks and a combination mechanism, the code for which **SHINE** had uploaded to her phone. EJ pulled back the bolt, used her skeleton key on the locks, turned the combination to 5-24-9-20, smiling as she realized what letters the numbers stood for. *That is the easiest number code*, she thought, as she pushed the door open and climbed up and onto the ground. As she shut the door, EJ could hear the train heading back to HQ. For EJ12, however, there was no turning back.

EJ took out her binoculars and compass and looked around to get her bearings. She was in a small clearing in the bush. Tall white gum trees stood all around her. EJ could smell the eucalyptus from the leaves and wondered if she might see a koala. When she looked to the south she could just make out the **SHINE** solar station in the distance through the trees, with its rows and rows of metallic panels pointing up to the sky. These were the panels that collected the sunlight. To the north, where EJ needed to go, there were more gum trees, a whole forest of them covering a small hill. If **SHINE** was right, Black Cave Mine was on the other side of that hill and the tower would be on the next hill.

The light of the day was fading, with the sun sinking lower and lower in the sky. Though it was still quite warm, a breeze was starting to blow gently, rustling the leaves. EJ knew from the position of the sun that it would be dark in less than thirty minutes. She began to make her way through the bush, eager to use the daylight while it lasted.

Dusk was a funny time. It wasn't quite day or night. When EJ was younger, she was sure that this was when fairies would come out. The last rays of sun were shining through the gum trees and in the dappled light EJ was almost sure that she saw the glisten of a fairy wing as it darted behind a tree. Or maybe that was just a butterfly. EJ never imagined scary things at this time of day, only magical, good things.

EJ's boots crunched as she stepped on leaves and fallen twigs. She hardly noticed the noise of her boots or of birds as they flapped and screeched around her. She pushed on, keeping her eyes on the compass to make sure she was going north. Only when her compass began to glow did EJ look up and realize it had become dark. The sun, which had been hovering just above the horizon, had suddenly dived down, throwing day into night, as if at the flick of a switch.

Now EJ noticed the noises.

She stepped forward and CRACK! She jumped back. What was that? She didn't dare take another step. Standing completely still, she felt for the zip of her light pack and rummaged inside. Grabbing the longest, biggest thing in there, she pulled out an enormous flashlight. She turned it on and shone it at her feet.

A stick. I stepped on a stick, she told herself. She shone the flashlight up at the trees. They had looked so pretty before with their speckled green-gray leaves dancing in the light. Now they were dark and shadowy, creaking and groaning as they bent in the wind. And there were noises everywhere. As well as the constant rustling of the leaves, there was a low buzzing.

"Crickets," said EJ to herself, as she walked on, "or frogs. I remember them from camp. They are quite nice when…"

wooooooooooooooooWIP!

EJ stopped and stood completely still when she heard the high-pitched, whipping noise ring through the bush. *That wasn't a frog*, she thought.

wooooooooooooooooWIP!

That wasn't a cricket. EJ swung her flashlight around but couldn't see anything.

woooooooooooooooooWIP!

The noise sounded closer. EJ's heart was pounding. What was that noise? That noise coming toward her... Toward her to attack? *Stay calm,* EJ said to herself. *It's only a bird or something ordinary like that. Remember the possum at home. This is just like that. The noise sounds scary, but it actually just belongs to a cute animal.* EJ shone the flashlight around again and this time, sitting on a high branch above her, she spotted a bird.

woooooooooooooooooWIP!

Mystery solved, thought EJ. *It is a bird, of course. Now stop thinking scary thoughts.* Then came another sound.

HOOOOOOOOOOO! HOOOOOOOOOOO!

"That's an owl," said EJ out loud. "You are a cute owl, aren't you?"

HOOOOOOOOOOOOOOOOO!

"Thanks," said EJ. "I knew you were." And so it went on as she walked through the bush. There would be a noise and EJ would tell herself what was making the noise, sensible things, not crazy, scary, spooky slumber party things. But there were noises everywhere and they seemed so close. EJ couldn't work out what they all were. She felt her heart start to beat fast again and she felt a warm flush run up her neck. She was starting to panic. EJ felt alone, she felt small and, most of all, she felt scared.

She wanted her mom.

CAAAWWWWWWWWWWWWWWRARARAR

Now EJ's heart was beating so hard she thought it was going to burst. *What is that? I need Mom!* EJ pressed the BEST app and her mom answered immediately.

"Hey, Em, I mean Agent EJ12. You'll do anything to get out of eating fish pie, won't you? I must say I'm not sure what I think about **SHINE** giving you a mission on a school night. I might email A1 about that."

"Mom, don't you dare!" said Emma, who was thinking her mom may not have been the right BESTie to choose after all. But the sound of her mom's voice made EJ feel calmer, safer. "Mom, there are some pretty scary noises here."

"Remember our possum at home," said her mom. "She made a pretty horrible noise but was actually very cute and not dangerous at all."

"I tried to remember that," said EJ, "but now there are so many weird noises, I'm not sure."

"Why don't you put me on speaker so I can hear too?" suggested Mom.

EJ was slightly surprised her mom knew phones had that but didn't say anything as she switched it on.

"Okay," said her mom, "let's keep walking."

And so EJ walked through the night bush chatting with her mom, who would sometimes say, "Oh that might be a sooty owl, EJ. Lucky you, they are very rare. Now that, I think, is a tawny frogmouth and that is definitely a barn owl."

And so it went on as EJ walked through the bush

and up the hill. She wasn't sure that her mom really knew the names of all the birds or whether she was making them up, but it didn't matter. She wasn't afraid anymore, she was even kind of enjoying it, and before long she had reached the top of the hill.

"Okay, Mom, thanks, I can do it myself now," said EJ.

"Of course you can. Good girl and good luck, EJ," said Mom, "and I'll save some fish pie for you."

EJ groaned but smiled as she put her phone back in her pocket. She must be getting close now. She needed to go down this hill and then the mine was on the next hill. And somewhere would be an entrance. As she headed down the other side of the hill, she could still hear noises, but EJ stayed calm. She knew they were just the bush animals and birds calling to each other. The ground had leveled out and then started to go up again. EJ checked her compass. She was still heading north so she must be nearly at the mine. EJ checked her sun charm. It had turned to a dark orange. That was not good, it meant that the **SHINE** energy supplies were getting dangerously low. She needed to hurry.

Chapter 7

As EJ walked, she shone the giant flashlight ahead of her, swinging it from side to side and up and down, looking for something that might be a mine entrance. Just as she was starting to think she would never find it, EJ felt her boots hit something. She shone the flashlight on the ground and saw a metal track, the mine cart track. She must be on the right track! Then EJ's flashlight shone on an old sign, nailed to a tree.

MINE CLOSED
DANGER
DO NOT PASS BEYOND THIS POINT

EJ had found an entrance to Black Cave Mine. She took a deep breath, held her flashlight out straight in front of her, and headed slowly down the track into the mine. EJ took one small, tentative step at a time, along the rusty, dusty track. Shining her flashlight around, EJ could see the tunnel's walls. They were made of deep red rock, with some smooth patches, some rough. EJ ran her hands along the wall and was surprised at how cold they felt.

EJ saw that the top of the tunnel wasn't much higher than her head and the tunnel floor was scattered with loose rocks between the cart tracks. She would have to watch her step.

Gee whizz, lemonfizz, it is dark in here, thought EJ. *Dark and cold. Maybe there is another way to find Operation Lights Out…*

Piinngg!

Saved by the Ping! It was another message from SHINE. EJ stopped and took out her phone. She looked at her screen.

```
SHADOW MESSAGE INTERCEPTED.
WAS IN BRAILLE.
CONVERTING FOR TRANSMISSION
SENDING NOW.
STAY WHERE YOU ARE.
```

SHADOW must have sent another message in Braille, thought EJ. *They can't send that to my phone.*

EJ was right. Because *SHADOW* had sent the first message in Braille, **SHINE** had been on the lookout—or should that be feel-out—for a second message using the same alphabet. So, when they intercepted what looked like a blank piece of paper, they checked for the little raised dots. They found them and then simply reproduced them digitally to send on to EJ.

Piinngg!

The message came through.

For EJ12's Eyes Only

Message Intercepted 18.21

Converted to Digital Braille 18.26

Urgent decode required.

They could have then converted it to the normal alphabet, couldn't they? thought EJ. *But then again, that is my job I suppose.*

EJ checked her code app and found the Braille alphabet again. In no time at all, she had converted the Braille to normal letters, but this time the message made no sense at all.

V E V I B G S R M T U R M V

N B G R N V G L H S R M V

O Z F M X S Z G M R M V

Z C

"It's obviously a code within a code," murmured EJ. "If I were a *SHADOW* agent hatching evil plans, what code would I use? That's hard, it's like the opposite of what I am, the complete opposite." *The opposite*, thought EJ. *Could that be it? SHINE— SHADOW; dark—light; good—bad; back—front… Hmm, could it be a backward code?*

EJ loved cracking codes. She loved taking something that looked like nonsense and working with it until it made sense. Now, looking at the letters, she had a feeling that she was about to crack this code.

Let's test it, thought EJ. *A backward code means A=Z and Z=A, B=Y and Y=B and it goes on like that, all the way through the alphabet. If the same SHADOW agent has signed off with her initials, AX, the last two letters of this code will be ZC.* EJ quickly checked. *Yes, they are. Backward code confirmed.* EJ flipped to the code app on her phone and found the decoder for the rest of the alphabet.

A	B	C	D	E	F	G	H
Z	Y	X	W	V	U	T	S
I	J	K	L	M	N	O	P
R	Q	P	O	N	M	L	K
Q	R	S	T	U	V	W	X
J	I	H	G	F	E	D	C
Y	Z						
B	A						

It took her no time at all to decode the rest of the message.

EVERYTHING FINE

MY TIME TO SHINE

LAUNCH AT NINE

AX

EJ keyed in the decoded message and sent it back to **SHINE**. Within seconds A1 was on the phone.

"Good work, EJ. Now we know that you have just two hours to stop AX."

"Do we know who AX is yet?" asked EJ.

"I think we do," replied A1. "There were thirteen *SHADOW* agents with the initials AX, but we have narrowed it down to two people, Adriana X or Alexandra X. Both are *SHADOW* agents, both have the skills to be behind something like this. We are sending you visuals of each now. There are, however, a few things that make us fairly sure that it is Adriana."

"What are they?" asked EJ.

"Well, the first thing is her name," said A1. "One of the meanings of the name Adriana is darkness. Someone with a name that means darkness being behind a plan to put **SHINE** in the dark, is that a coincidence, I wonder? I do not think so, I really don't."

"And the other things?" asked EJ.

"The code," said A1, "the use of the Braille alphabet and the poetry. We know Adriana has very bad eyesight. She can hardly see a thing. That might explain the Braille. And the poetry, if you can call those bad rhymes poetry, well, Adriana always fancied herself as a poet. No one else did, I might add, but she often sends messages in rhyme. It is almost like her trademark. It's been a while since we have heard from Adriana, but this kind of scheme is just the sort of thing she might get up to."

"How do we know so much about her?" asked EJ.

"Adriana has caused quite a few problems for **SHINE** over the years," sighed A1.

"But how would she know where the solar station is?" asked EJ. "Isn't that top secret? How could Adriana have found that out?"

"I'm afraid I can't tell you that, EJ," said A1. "It's classified information with the highest security clearance required on a strictly need-to-know basis. I can tell you however, that if it is Adriana who is behind Operation Lights Out, she does know where the solar station is and how it works. Now, you need to get down that mine, and you need to hurry. And remember, EJ, make sure you can't be seen."

EJ looked down the mine tunnel. She could see only blackness. She gulped.

"That shouldn't be hard," she said.

Chapter 8

EJ sat down in the tunnel and took out her tub of face concealer. She put her flashlight on the ground, opened the tub and smeared the black cream on her face, then did a quick check in the mirror under the lid of the tub. She could hardly see herself. It was perfect.

As she got up she accidentally kicked the flashlight and sent it crashing into the tunnel's rock wall. There was a cracking noise and EJ was in complete darkness—she had broken her flashlight. She sat on the ground, trying to think her way out of feeling really, really scared.

Okay, so it is a little dark, okay very dark, but so what? EJ told herself. *What's so bad about that?*

"Oh, I can tell you," she answered her own question, her heart starting to pound again. "How about spiders, snakes, tunnels caving in, crazy SHADOW agents creeping up on you…"

"Stop it," said EJ out loud. "You're doing it again. Remember what A1 said. Don't let your imagination run away with you. 'Shine a light on your fears.' I need to see to do that, so let's just get something else from the light bag on the ground next to me. Here? No, here? No." EJ groped around frantically trying to find the black backpack in the darkness. She could feel the dirt, some rock, but no bag. She stretched her hands out and touched a strap. EJ pulled the bag toward her and felt around inside. She knew what she was searching for and when her hand touched a narrow case, she pulled it out. Opening the case, EJ took out the night-vision glasses. She put them on and flicked the switch on the side of the glasses. Immediately she could see about ten yards around her, all through the red glare of the night-vision glasses.

I may have lost my flashlight, thought EJ, looking on the bright side, *but these leave my hands free and I can see better with them.* EJ felt a little proud of herself and she was sure her mom would be very proud.

With her glasses on, EJ immediately found her flashlight, or what was left of it. She leaned down and hit the Eco-Deco button on the base of the handle. Eco-Deco was another **SHINE** invention that got rid of mission equipment once it was broken or finished with. All **SHINE** gear was made from materials that could decompose. The agent simply pushed a button and the piece of equipment would break down. No one would ever know that the agent had been there and it was good for the environment. There was one downside, however. The process was quite noisy in a farty, burpy kind of way and, as you would expect from those noises, quite smelly as well. With some of the larger equipment it could be explosive. Even with something the size of a flashlight, EJ knew better than to hang around. She picked up her backpack and walked off down the tunnel. Even a long, dark tunnel would be better than the smell that was about to come.

Now that she could see better, EJ was half wishing she couldn't. The first thing she saw was cobwebs and cobwebs meant spiders. She really, really didn't like spiders, especially the ones that were hairy and crawly. She was scared of them the way some people were scared of snakes or mice. Even the ones that she knew weren't dangerous, like daddy longlegs, scared her. She always imagined them crawling on her. Yuk!

EJ ran her hands along the rock walls of the tunnel as she walked and they felt hard and cold. Down in the tunnel the air smelled musty and with no wind it was completely still. It was so different from walking in the dark outside in the bush. EJ almost missed the bird and animal noises. The complete silence made her feel really alone. But she wasn't alone because somewhere in the mine was Adriana or Alexandra hard at work on turning **SHINE's** lights out. Hardly a comforting thought.

The tunnel suddenly split into two paths. *Which one to take?* EJ wondered. She took the path to the right and had walked some way when she found it blocked by a large slab of fallen rock. *Not too large though,* thought EJ, as she pushed on the rock, feeling it give a bit under her weight. Another push and she felt it lift a little. With a third really big push, EJ rolled the rock over and off the track. As the rock lifted, spiders rushed out, scattering. It seemed like there were hundreds of them scuttling toward EJ. She jumped back with a scream.

EJ stood there, frozen, staring at the stream of spiders. There was no way she could get past them. She fiddled with her charm bracelet, as she often did when she was nervous, or thinking. Now, because she was both, she was fiddling a lot, which was when she noticed one of the new charms, the little ladybug. *What does that one do?* she wondered. *Might it help?* She took out her phone and was about to check her animal app when she noticed a new app on her phone screen.

SHINE
CHARM GUIDE

That's a good idea, thought EJ, as she scrolled down the charms. *It takes some of the guesswork out of using them*. All of the hundreds of **SHINE** charms were listed with little pictures and explanations of what they could do. There was a dolphin, a guitar, an ice cream cone, and, *hmmm, a cupcake…* She wondered if you could order them for future use. Then she came to the one she needed right now.

LADYBUG SPIDERS AWAY
SPIDER DETERRENT SPRAY. ONE
TWIST PER USE, CLOSE TO TARGET.
5 TWISTS PER LADYBUG.
RECHARGEABLE.

Perfect! Well, nearly. The instructions said you had to use the charm close to the spiders. EJ took a deep breath and, making sure she was leaning over the center of the swarm, twisted the charm.

Hiiiiiiiiiiiiiiiiiiiiiiiiiiiiiiiiiiiiissssssssssssssssssssssssssssssss

A cloud of smelly smoke came out of the ladybug and EJ watched the spiders rush away, moving back into the rocks at the side of the path. After a few moments, with almost all of the spiders gone, EJ could continue. Now the path kept turning and EJ kept walking. As she did, she got the feeling that something wasn't quite right. Then she thought she could smell the ladybug smoke again. She could. EJ's heart sank when she saw the rock she had moved and a few last spiders scrambling into rock crevices. She had gone in a complete circle.

What a waste of time, thought EJ.

She looked down at her sun charm, which had turned from a light orange to a deeper, redder color. Adriana or Alexandra and Operation Lights Out were somewhere in this mine, but would she ever find it if she kept walking in circles?

EJ needed a plan, and quickly.

Chapter •9

EJ needed something to mark her path so she would know if she was doubling back, but what would work in darkness? Could she leave a trail of rocks behind her? Even with night-vision glasses it would be hard to see them and one rock looked pretty much like another. That wouldn't work. *But what would?* wondered EJ. EJ looked down at her charm bracelet. Would one of the new charms be able to help her make some kind of marking? Then EJ remembered her mission briefing. She had been given a charm that looked like a piece of string. That could be something. Again, she opened the charm app on her phone and flicked through the charm listings.

GLOW STRING
IF YOU CAN'T SEE A THING, USE YOUR GLOW STRING!
3000 FEET.
KEEP OUT OF REACH OF PETS.

EJ twisted the charm and, as she did, string poked out from it. The string was thin but extremely tough and better still, it glowed. The more EJ pulled the glow string, the more it came out. EJ looked around and found a large rock, tied the string around it and then walked away, feeding the string out and leaving a thin but bright glowing trail behind her. She headed down the tunnel and this time, when she came to the fork in the path, she went to the left. As she turned, she checked the string. It was still feeding out. EJ felt better knowing that not only would she not double back on herself, but she would also be able to go back if she needed to. That was comforting as she traveled deeper into the mine.

Suddenly, as EJ turned another corner, she thought she could hear music. EJ checked her phone, thinking she may have accidentally turned on her music app, but it was off. She continued walking and the tunnel began to turn again, and there it was again, the music, this time getting louder. If there was music, surely there was someone listening to it. Adriana? Alexandra? It had to be. And if EJ could hear it she must be getting close.

And then there was another noise.

EooooooooOOOOOW

EJ spun around. *What is that?* As she spun, she was still feeding the string out. She twisted it around herself and fell to the ground. Her glasses were knocked off and, except for the thin line that was her glow string, EJ could see nothing. Once again she groped around. She couldn't feel anything but dirt. Slowly, feeling the tunnel wall, she stood up and took a step forward. As she did, she heard a cracking, crunching sound. The cracking, crunching sound of glass.

Please don't tell me I've stepped on my night-vision glasses, thought EJ. She crouched down again and felt around on the ground. As soon as she touched the glasses she could tell they were ruined. She felt for the button on the side, flicked it, and Eco-Deco swung into smelly action. In just a few minutes there would be nothing left of the night-vision glasses.

At least there was still the mini flashlight in her light bag. EJ pulled the bag off her back, rifled around inside and found the slim flashlight. She shone it around the tunnel, but she could barely see a step ahead of her. EJ moved slowly, one hand out in front of her and the other running along the tunnel wall, listening, trying to follow the music.

EooooooOOOOOOW

That wasn't music.

Eoooooooooooooow

EJ gulped and stopped. What could that noise be? A ghost? EJ shuddered. *Ghosts aren't real,* she thought. *It's just your imagination. Stop thinking about it.*

But she couldn't, and then there it was again.

Eooooooooooooow

"It can't be something that doesn't exist, it can't be a ghost, it just can't," said EJ out loud to herself, and then she heard the music again. For a moment she was distracted. She could hear the music clearly now and, unless EJ was mistaken, it was "Getting Dark," the latest song from one of the most popular bands, the Pink Shadows.

Eooooooooooooooooooooooow

But there was that other noise again. The scary it-can't-be-a-ghost noise.

As EJ twisted around to face the direction of the sound, she stumbled and dropped her flashlight.

Her last flashlight. There was no light now except the thin glow of the string. She felt for the string, but this time as she moved it, something pulled back. Something was pulling the string. Or someone.

Then, as EJ stood still, she saw them in the darkness.

A pair of eyes.

A pair of green, glowing eyes.

A pair of green, glowing eyes coming toward EJ. And as EJ pulled the string, whatever the eyes belonged to seemed to pull it back.

EJ's heart pounded so hard she was sure it was going to jump right out of her chest. And then there was that noise again, louder and coming from the direction of the green, glowing eyes.

Eooooooooooooow

EJ was frozen. "I don't believe in ghosts, I don't believe in ghosts," she muttered to herself breathlessly and completely unconvincingly. As the green eyes came closer and the sound became even louder, EJ felt sick.

Chapter •10

EJ had to do something besides feeling sick. Green Eyes was coming closer, tugging on the string. EJ wriggled against the wall of the tunnel, knocking some rocks loose as she did.

Hiiiiiiiiiiiiiiiiiiiiiiiiiiiiiiiiiiiiiiiiiiiiissssssssssssssssssssssssssss!

Green Eyes didn't like that, thought EJ.

EooooooooooooooooooooooooOW

Now EJ thought she felt something push ever

so lightly against her leg. She couldn't see the eyes anymore. Where had they gone? And what was that new noise?

Uuuurrrrrrrrrrrrrrrrrrrr, urrrrrrrrrrrrrrrrrrrrr

It was like a machine. What was this thing? A mechanical ghost? And what was it doing, whatever it was?

EJ was terrified. She felt for her pack, unzipped it and stretched her hand down to the bottom, feeling for the matchbox and candle. She pulled the box out, slowly took out a match and struck it. Holding the match, EJ took out the candle and lit it. The flame flickered and cast a small glow. As she blew out the match, she noticed the heart charm with the candle. Would that give her some more light? She hoped so. EJ twisted it and as she did, an inscription appeared.

Shine a light on your fears.

It was the motto A1 had told her.

Eooooooooooooooooooooooooooooooow

That's easy for you to say, A1, thought EJ, but she decided to give it a try. *Shine a light on my fears.* EJ held the candle out toward the noise and gasped. She couldn't believe what she was looking at.

Two green eyes.

Two green eyes and black fur.

If it hadn't been dark and if she hadn't been wearing face concealer, you would've been able to see EJ go red. She had just been spooked by a kitten, jet-black but for its white paws. A kitten with a long piece of EJ's glow string in its claws. That was the tugging EJ had felt on her string. She could see that the kitten must have clawed right through the string tied around the rock and was now playing with it.

"Eoooooowwwwwww," said the kitten.

"How embarrassing," said EJ. "But you are pretty cute even if you did scare the life out of me," she said to the kitten, who kept rubbing against her leg, purring. Now the "urrrrrrrrrrrrrrrrrrrrrr, urrrrrrrrrrrrrrrrrrrrrrrrr" didn't seem like a machine at all. It sounded like a fluffy, happy kitten. How could she have thought it was anything else?

"Why do you have to have such scary eyes?" she asked the little cat. "Where are you from and what have you done to my string?" The kitten purred as EJ stroked its back. EJ rolled up what was left of her string. There would be no retracing her steps now. EJ started walking in the direction of the music again. "Are you coming with me?" she asked. The kitten purred and padded behind her. The music was really loud now and EJ could also hear someone singing along, although not very well.

The tunnel turned again and suddenly seemed to lighten. The further along EJ walked, the louder the music got and the lighter the tunnel became. Had EJ found the light at the end of the tunnel? Was it Operation Lights Out?

EJ blew out her candle. She didn't want to be seen as she edged closer to the light. Creeping along close to the ground, she tried to make herself as small and as flat as she could. She saw some large pieces of rock close to where the tunnel widened. Hoping there wouldn't be any more spiders there, EJ hid behind it and watched. In her black gear and with her black face concealer she was impossible to see. She hoped.

★ ★ ★

The tunnel had widened out to become what looked like a room. It was one of the landings she had seen in the drawing of the mine's tunnel system. At the far end of the landing was a large cage attached to heavy wires that went straight up into the darkness. *That must be the mine shaft elevator,* thought EJ.

To the left of the elevator was darkness, but to the right there was a large spotlight in the corner, shining on a lab bench that ran the length of the wall. On the bench were computer screens and panels filled with buttons and flashing lights. Everything seemed connected to what looked like a giant battery sitting under the bench and above it was an enormous screen. It was like the **SHINE** Light Screen, with lots of images flashing. They were all pictures of some kind of factory. As EJ watched, images of rows and rows of large panels facing up to the sun appeared. It was the **SHINE** solar power station. This had to be Operation Lights Out.

Then shuffling out of the shadows, singing badly to herself, came a woman. She looked older than EJ's mom but not quite as old as her grandma. She was wearing a long black coat with pockets over-flowing with pieces of paper. She was also wearing the thickest pair of black-rimmed glasses EJ had ever seen, not that they seemed to be doing much good as she kept bumping into things. Around her neck was a long silver chain with a black pendant and she had shiny, jet-black hair swept up in a rather messy bun. Sticking out of the bun, in a way that reminded EJ of something (or was it someone?), were pens, pencils and a small ruler. EJ knew from the **SHINE** visuals that this woman was Adriana.

Eoooooooooooooow

"Sssh!" whispered EJ, a little too loudly.

Adriana turned around sharply. "What's that I hear? Is someone near?"

Chapter •11

Adriana turned off the music and shuffled toward the tunnel, squinting through her glasses. EJ put her head down. She didn't like her chances of not being seen. She could hear the shuffling coming closer. Just as she was sure she was about to be discovered, the kitten ran out of the tunnel and up to Adriana.

"Oh, it is only you, Inky-poo, I wondered where you had gotten to. You mustn't run away from Adriana. It's bad, it makes me sad," she said, stroking the kitten. "And we have to get ready to go—it's nearly time for the show."

Why does she talk in bad rhymes? wondered EJ. *And what is the show?*

"What is the show?" asked Adriana.

Did I say that out loud? wondered EJ, but then, as she raised her head slightly, she could see that Adriana was talking to the kitten.

"The show—the final part of Operation Lights Out. The part when all in *SHADOW* shout, 'Adriana, you are the best!' But first, I must run the test."

She's crazy! thought EJ, watching intently as Adriana put Inky down and shuffled toward the computer monitors. She peered at a screen, furiously typing on the keyboard as she did and talking in her funny rhymes.

"Hurrah, the energy levels are so, so low, there's not much more to go! In just a sec, in just a mo, it will be time for Eco-Deco!"

Eco-Deco? thought EJ. *That's a SHINE invention. How would Adriana know about that and what is she using it for?* EJ shifted her legs slightly and, as she did, her feet knocked some rocks, scattering them loudly against the tunnel wall. Adriana heard the noise and this time the kitten couldn't save EJ. Adriana pointed the giant spotlight into the tunnel and onto EJ.

"Well, that makes my day. I've found an EJ," laughed Adriana.

For the first time all mission, EJ12 wished she was still in the dark.

$$\star \; \bigstar \; \star$$

EJ was now sitting on a chair with her hands tied behind her back with her own string.

Adriana said, "I should have known A1 would send someone like you. Well, now her plan has fallen through."

"A1, what is A1? I don't know what you're talking about," said EJ, acting surprised. The identity of all SHINE agents, but particularly A1, was closely guarded. Agents were trained never to reveal another agent's code name.

"Cut it out, EJ12," said Adriana, suddenly dropping

the poetry and looking very serious and very mean. "I know all about **SHINE**, about A1, your Light Screen and your charms. In fact, I invented a few."

"You what?" gasped EJ.

"Didn't your precious A1 tell you, EJ12? No, I suppose she wouldn't. 'Need-to-know basis,' I suppose she said. Well, I used to be a **SHINE** agent. I was one of the best, almost the best except for her."

"Her? Who?" asked EJ.

"A1, of course, do keep up!" Adriana snapped. "I was always second to A1, second in the Shining Stars, second in sports, my code name was even A2. I got tired of always being in A1's shadow. She was always hogging the limelight, like a typical older sister. Hmmph! Older by only three minutes."

EJ nearly choked. "You are A1's *twin* sister?"

"Yes, can't you see the resemblance? I'm the beautiful one, of course, but Aurora does have a few of my striking features."

And now, as EJ looked, she could see it. That was what Adriana's hair had reminded her of—it was

A1. Adriana's hair may have been black and A1's was white, but otherwise it was almost identical, all the way down to the pencils. And, now that she looked, their faces had a similar shape too. And they even both had pendants. EJ stared, her mouth open in disbelief.

"You can close your mouth now," said Adriana. "Is it really that hard to believe? But of course everyone always said Aurora was the beautiful one, the clever one. 'Why don't you be like Aurora?' our teachers would say. 'She's such a shining example!' Blah, blah, blah. And at **SHINE** it was the same thing all over again. No one seemed to notice that I could do things, like write poetry, and invent things, clever things. But my poetry was laughed at and my inventions never got the praise they deserved, some never even got to see the light of day. So I left and went where my talents were appreciated. *SHADOW* valued me. They put me in the spotlight, where I belong. And now it will be *SHADOW* and I who turn the lights out on Aurora and her precious **SHINE** with my brilliant invention. Oh yes," hissed

Adriana, leaning closer to EJ, staring straight into her eyes, "it will be so fine, to turn the lights out now on SHINE!"

Chapter •12

EJ was struggling to keep up with what she was learning. A1's name was Aurora? Adriana was her evil twin sister? Adriana had been a **SHINE** agent but was now working for *SHADOW*? All because she was jealous? And what was her invention?

"Brilliant invention?" asked EJ.

"Yes, you midget, I suppose it can't hurt to tell you. I, Adriana X, have invented an invisible shadow."

"To do what?"

"To secretly block the sun, of course. Don't be so dim, EJ12. There is a pole running up the mine shaft that is attached to a powerful ray gun positioned at the top of the tower. The ray gun shoots out tiny, microscopic particles to create an invisible shadow, which blocks the sun from reaching SHINE's solar panels. It's like a woman-made cloud."

"But how can something that is invisible block anything?" asked EJ12.

"Thank heavens I left SHINE!" exclaimed Adriana. "I couldn't bear to be surrounded by such stupidity, and by such small people. The cloud only *looks* invisible. That is where I have outdone myself. Any scientist can whip up a cloud, even SHINE could, but my cloud is color-tinted to match the color of the sky, so when those silly SHINE engineers look up, all they think they see is clear blue sky. And while they've been scratching their heads, the SHINE power levels have been dropping. Now SHINE is almost completely out of power."

"That's Operation Lights Out?" said EJ.

"Clever you, you intercepted my message did you?" replied Adriana. "Then you will also know I have another little surprise for SHINE."

"The blast."

"Exactly. When the energy levels hit zero, the whole plant will be destroyed. It will decompose, break down to absolutely nothing."

"You can't do that," shouted EJ.

"Actually, I won't have to do a thing. **SHINE** will do it all to itself. Shall I illuminate you? When the energy levels hit zero the whole plant will go into Eco-Deco mode. It will decompose, to nothing. I invented Eco-Deco and I put it in everything I make. E-D, Eco-Deco, don't you like the poetic touch? I like to think of it as my parting gift to Aurora, to have put Eco-Deco into the solar plant without her knowing. But don't look so sad, EJ, there will be some super, if rather smelly fireworks. According to my calculations, it will all happen at nine o'clock. Oh yes, at nine o'clock, the place will rock!"

"Can't you see that what you are doing is wrong?" said EJ.

"Haven't you noticed, EJ 'zero,'" said Adriana, "that I can't see very much at all and soon neither will anyone else at **SHINE**. I'd love to stay and chat some more, but I really must fly. My *SHADOW* helicopter is waiting for me at the top of the mine tower. I don't want to miss the fireworks, the last show of light before **SHINE** plunges into darkness. So if you will excuse me I just need to…" Adriana walked over to her computer and tapped some keys. "Perhaps you would like to watch the countdown?" asked Adriana, turning the screen toward EJ.

```
TIME TO ZERO ENERGY:
15 MINS 00 SECS
```

Adriana shuffled over to the elevator and opened the door. But before she got in, she turned back to EJ.

"Good-bye, EJ12. I am sure my goody-goody sister will come and rescue you, eventually, but you don't mind if I turn the lights out, do you? I wouldn't want to waste electricity. I'd like to stay but must away. Better luck next time, little EJ!"

And with that, Adriana laughed a mean cackle of a laugh and flicked the light switch. The entire cave went dark. EJ could hear the clang of the cage door open and then another clang as it shut and then a whirring noise as the elevator shot up the mine shaft. Adriana had gone and EJ was left alone, tied up in the dark.

Chapter •13

Even if she had been able to move, EJ wouldn't have wanted to. She would have been too afraid that she would bump into something, something dangerous, something scary. If only she could have reached her phone, she could have used the BEST system. Now, more than ever, she could really have used another talk with Mom.

Her mom would have told her that the scary blowing noise she could hear was just the wind whirling around the mine shaft. Her mom would have told her that the spooky dim glow in the corner was just the glow of the computer screens. EJ thought her mom might also have suggested she stop imagining scary things and start trying to escape and save the solar station.

That jolted EJ out of her thoughts. She didn't even stop to realize that she had just "un-scared" herself. Instead, she looked over at the screen.

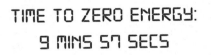

TIME TO ZERO ENERGY:
9 MINS 57 SECS

Eooooooooooooow

Now that's a noise I know, thought EJ. The sound that was so scary before was now a relief to EJ. It told her that she was no longer alone.

"Hey, Inky, Adriana was supposed to take you with her," said EJ to the kitten that was brushing against her legs.

The kitten walked around the chair and stretched up to reach EJ's hands.

"I can't stroke you, I'm kind of tied up right now," said EJ, pleased with her ability to make a joke at a difficult time. "Hey, cut that out!" she cried, as the kitten clawed playfully at her hands. "Your claws are sharp." And then EJ had an idea. Inky had clawed through the string once already, back in the tunnel, so why not again?

"Inky, Inky, up here," cried EJ, jiggling her hands as much as she could, hoping the kitten would think it was a game. She did. The kitten stretched up, clawing at the string. EJ kept jiggling her hands and Inky kept trying to catch them with her claws. It wasn't long before she had clawed little rips in the string, enough for EJ to break through the rest. EJ's hands were free, a little scratched but free. "Well done, Inky," said EJ.

She untied her feet, stood up and slowly made her way over toward the dim glow of the computer screens. As she approached, she could see they all showed the same thing.

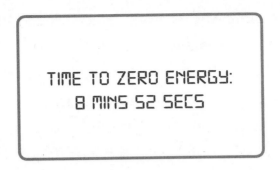

TIME TO ZERO ENERGY:
8 MINS 52 SECS

Think, EJ, think! How can I stop the plant reaching zero energy and Eco-Deco going off?

EJ took out her phone to search for an app that could help her, but when she opened it, the screen flashed a warning.

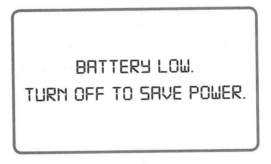

BATTERY LOW.
TURN OFF TO SAVE POWER.

"Oh no!" exclaimed EJ, but then said, "That's it! Turn everything off. That's how it can be stopped. If **SHINE** turns everything off, no more energy will be used, the plant won't reach zero energy and Eco-Deco will be a no go! Oh, I am turning into Adriana—I'm a poet and I know it," said EJ, laughing to herself. She sent a text to **SHINE HQ**. There was enough battery power for that.

> PLANT SET FOR ECO-DECO.
> TURN OFF EVERYTHING.

EJ waited, hoping.

Piinngg!

> OKAY EJ.
> SHINE IN THE DARK.

EJ watched the computer screen closely. She knew she was running out of time. Had her plan worked?

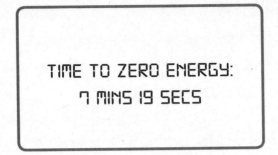

TIME TO ZERO ENERGY:
7 MINS 19 SECS

Then

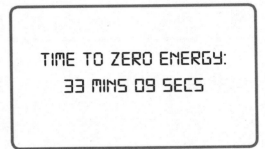

TIME TO ZERO ENERGY:
33 MINS 09 SECS

And then

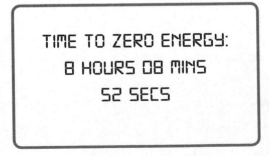

TIME TO ZERO ENERGY:
8 HOURS 08 MINS
52 SECS

The time to zero energy was increasing. With **SHINE** shut down, the plant was saving its power. Adriana shouldn't have underestimated EJ12. She had done it—she had stopped Eco-Deco. The plant would now have enough power to keep above zero and in the morning would begin to recharge with the sunlight. With Adriana gone, the invisible cloud wouldn't be turned on. Or would it? EJ12 had one more thing to do.

EJ needed to shut down Adriana's lab—but quickly before Adriana realized her plan had failed and came back.

If only I could Eco-Deco the lab, EJ thought. *Hold on, can't I?* She remembered what Adriana had said: "I put it in everything I make." So did she put an ED button on the ray gun? ED buttons on her screens? EJ looked across to the shaft, then, realizing that she was still in the dark, reached up to the wall, felt for the light switch and turned it on. *That's better*, she thought. *Now where are all those ED buttons?*

EJ looked behind the screens and, sure enough, there were little ED buttons. In fact, now that she was looking for them, there were buttons everywhere. She ran over to the shaft and on the back of the pole there was another ED button. EJ checked the time. It was nearly nine o'clock and Adriana would be expecting fireworks. Well, she would get them, but she might be surprised where they came from!

EJ ran to the computers and pressed the ED buttons, she pressed more buttons under the table, she pressed the button under the large screen then she scooped up Inky and ran to the mine shaft. EJ stretched out and pressed the button on the pole of the ray gun. Already she could hear the farting noises starting. She needed to get out of the mine fast, but the elevator was at the top of the tower. The noises were getting louder. Her boots, of course. EJ clicked her boots. Roller blades came out. EJ clicked again and riding boots appeared.

"I don't have time for this," cried EJ, getting frustrated. "I need the jet packs."

She clicked again. Yes! The jet packs came out at the back of EJ's boots. She pulled the laces and the jet packs roared into life, nearly tipping EJ over as they started to lift her up. EJ had to be careful to keep her balance and keep holding on to Inky.

"Up we go, Inky. This is going to be pretty fast," cried EJ, scooping up the kitten as she pulled the laces again to kick up into turbo charge.

Like a flash, EJ shot up the mine shaft, out of the mine and into the night sky. With some skillful maneuvering she brought herself down onto the hill overlooking the mine. As she landed, she could see the SHADOW chopper in the distance, hovering above the SHINE power station.

"Adriana is waiting for her fireworks," said EJ, as she sat on the top of the hill, stroking Inky, who was now sitting in her lap, purring. "If I am not mistaken the show is just about to begin." EJ turned back to watch the mine tower as she heard the first, familiar noises of Eco-Deco in action.

BUUUURRRRRRRP

KABOOM!

A shock of fireworks shot out of the mine. They were pink and purple, blue and white, fizzing and whizzing high into the sky. Adriana was right, it was quite a show.

EJ watched with amusement as the *SHADOW* chopper spun around and started flying over to the mine tower. Then it stopped, spun around again and flew quickly away. **SHINE** might have stopped Adriana's plan, but they weren't going to catch her this time.

The chopper had nearly disappeared from view when...

Piinngg!

A text. That was quick of A1, thought EJ, as she flipped open her phone.

> JUST A MINOR SETBACK,
> I'LL BE FINE.
> NEXT TIME I WILL
> OUTSMART SHINE.

How did she know my number? wondered EJ.

Piinngg!

> I KNOW EVERYTHING.

"Oh no, not two of them!" cried EJ.

Chapter •14

EJ sat on the hill enjoying the last of the fireworks, but it had been a long night and she was tired. It was time to go home. She took out her phone and pressed 4-6-6-3 into the keypad and a woman's voice answered immediately.

"**SHINE** Home Delivery Service—straight to your door anytime, anywhere."

"Agent EJ12 requesting home delivery," replied EJ. Looking at the little kitten now asleep on her lap, she added, "For two, again." EJ had a habit of collecting animals on her missions.

"Roger that. We are on standby in the area, EJ12. Stay where you are. Estimated pickup time, five minutes."

By the time the pickup helicopter arrived EJ was almost falling asleep. She held Inky tight as she climbed aboard. Agent LP30 greeted her.

"Good evening, EJ12, and congratulations on another mission well done. I have A1 on standby waiting to talk to you. Please put on your headphones."

EJ did and when she heard A1's voice, she was surprised how similar it was to Adriana's. Was it Adriana?

"We do sound similar, don't we, EJ? But you can be assured it is me, A1. So now you know the stories are true and you have met my confused sister, Adriana. I had hoped we would be able to catch her and try to reason with her, but her helicopter moved quickly once she saw her plan was foiled. Maybe next time."

"I think she has other ideas," said EJ.

"I'm sure she does," replied A1, "but let's not

worry about that now, let's look on the bright side. You've saved the power station. In a few days, our energy supplies will be back to normal. Well done, EJ12."

"Thank you," said EJ, trying to stop herself yawning.

"Yes, you must be tired. Sit back and snooze, we will have you home in no time. And don't worry about an early start. We have arranged with your mom to write a late note for school tomorrow."

Mom? That made EJ think of something. "A1, can you please send a message to Mom?"

"My pleasure, EJ. What's the message?"

"Would you mind asking if she was really serious when she said I couldn't have any more pets…"

"Will do. And one more thing, EJ. EJ?"

EJ didn't answer. She had fallen asleep.

Back home on the weekend, Emma was fully rested after her mission. Pip and Inky were chasing each other around the backyard—Emma's mom had been sort of understanding about Inky—while Emma was getting ready for the slumber party. She had packed her bag with everything she needed, including a skeleton mask and an enormous bag of candy, and put her pillow and Floppy on top of the bag by the front door. Elle's mom would be there any minute to pick her up and take them both to Hannah's house.

"Are you going to be okay?" said Mom, coming up behind Emma, putting her arms around her and giving her a squeeze.

"What do you mean, Mom?" asked Emma.

"Well, you know, are you worried about the slumber party and the scary stories and maybe being a bit nervous in the dark?"

"Not anymore, Mom. I could do it with my eyes closed!"

Her mom smiled, then the doorbell rang and Emma ran to the door. It was Elle and Isi and both of them were excited. Isi was possibly overexcited. She hugged Emma so hard that Emma could hardly breathe.

"This will be so much fun," cried Isi and then, whispering into Emma's ear added, "but, Em, if I get a bit scared, will you look after me? You don't seem to be scared of anything."

Isi got scared too? Emma smiled before whispering back, "Of course I will, we can look after each other."

"Grab your stuff, Em," said Elle. "We are going to have the scariest, best slumber party ever. Are you ready?"

"Are you kidding?" cried Emma. "Of course I am!"

And she was, thanks to a little help from EJ12.

Emma Jacks and EJ12 will return in

BOOK 4
ROCKY ROAD

Did you miss Book 1?

The heat is on as someone seems to be melting the polar ice cap.

Special Agent EJ12 needs to crack the codes and keep her cool to put the evildoer's plan back on ice.
That's the easy part.

As EJ12, Emma Jacks can do anything.

So why can't she handle the school Ice Queen of Mean, Nema?

Perhaps she can after all...

Book 2!

EJ12 GIRL HERO

JUMP START

Evil agency SHADOW is up to something in the middle of the rain forest. Something that could see them get the jump on SHINE.

Special Agent EJ12 needs to leap into action. She must crack SHADOW's codes and trust her instincts to foil their plans and save the rain forest.

That's the easy part.
As EJ12, Emma Jacks can do anything.

So why is the state gymnastics meet so hard?

Perhaps it isn't after all...